PATCHES
Finds a Home

This Book Belongs To:

by Vanessa Giancamilli   Illustrated by Dan Hatala

_____

A Gift From
Delta Kappa Gamma
&
Reading is Fundamental

AMERICAN VETERINARY MEDICAL ASSOCIATION ®

To Wilson, because all dogs come into a person's life for a reason. — V.G.

Book copyright © 2006 Trudy Corporation

Published by Soundprints Division of Trudy Corporation, Norwalk, Connecticut.

All rights reserved. No part of this book may be reproduced or transmitted in any form or by any means whatsoever without prior written permission of the publisher.

Book design: Marcin D. Pilchowski
Editor: Barbie Schwaeber
Production Editor: Brian E. Giblin

First Edition 2006
10 9 8 7 6 5 4 3 2 1
Printed in China

Acknowledgements:
   Soundprints would like to thank the staff at the American Veterinary Medical Association and its member veterinarians who assisted in reviewing the story and illustrations.

PATCHES
Finds a Home

by Vanessa Giancamilli   Illustrated by Dan Hatala

Soundprints

A beautiful young black-and-tan dog wakes up in the morning. He lives at a large, clean shelter with many other animals. Lots of caretakers and Dr. Flannagan, the shelter's veterinarian, take care of the animals that are waiting to be adopted by nice families.

When he first arrived at the shelter, the black-and-tan dog had visited Dr. Flannagan for a check-up. She looked in his ears and examined his teeth. She also gave him special vaccines to protect against illnesses. He is now healthy and eager to be adopted.

The dog is in luck — today is a special Pet Adoption Day! The black-and-tan dog would love to find a home. He has seen many other animals, adopted by nice people and he wants to be part of a family too!

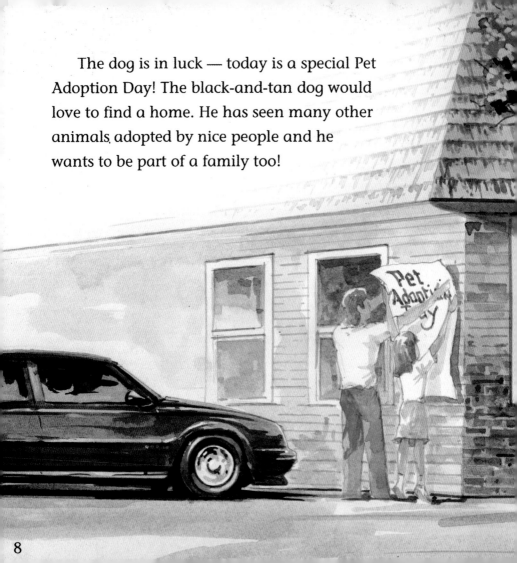

9

The black-and-tan dog enjoys a nutritious meal after being taken outside for his morning run. A member of the shelter staff gives him a bath and brushes his coat until it shines. He will look his very best today.

Many people visit the shelter during Pet Adoption Day and several think they see the perfect pets for their families. A few people stop to look at the black-and-tan dog, but no one asks to adopt him. It is the end of the day and the dog is sad. He is sure nobody wants him.

Then, one last family comes through the shelter. A young boy named Henry stops to look at the dog. Henry kneels down and pets him. The dog's tail wags with excitement. Henry wants to take him home! Henry and his parents promise to take very good care of the black-and-tan dog. They have a big, fenced yard where he can run and play.

Dr. Flannagan and the shelter caretakers are very happy the dog will live in a good home with a nice family.

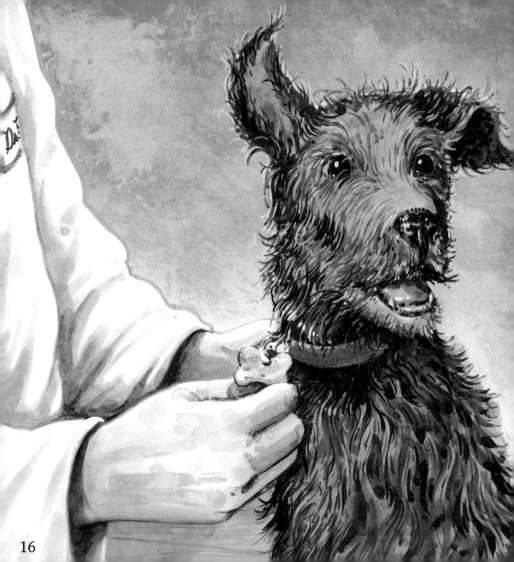

Before Henry and his family can take their new dog home, they must give him a name so the shelter caretaker can put a tag on the dog's collar. Henry's parents let him name their new pet. Henry names him Patches. The shelter caretaker gives Patches a red tag shaped like a bone for his collar.

Henry and his family are well prepared for Patches to live with them. Henry is excited as he leads Patches up the stairs into his home for the first time.

19

Even though Patches is happy in his new home, he is a little shy. But every night before Henry goes to bed, he gently pets Patches and tells the dog that he will be loved forever.

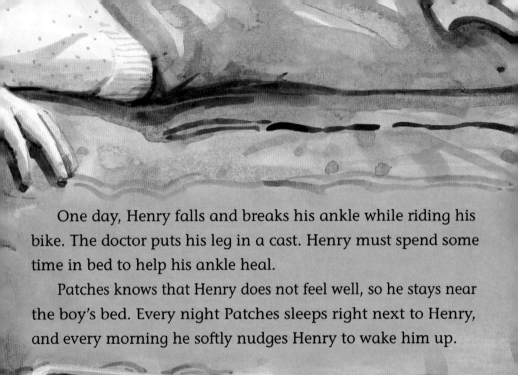

One day, Henry falls and breaks his ankle while riding his bike. The doctor puts his leg in a cast. Henry must spend some time in bed to help his ankle heal.

Patches knows that Henry does not feel well, so he stays near the boy's bed. Every night Patches sleeps right next to Henry, and every morning he softly nudges Henry to wake him up.

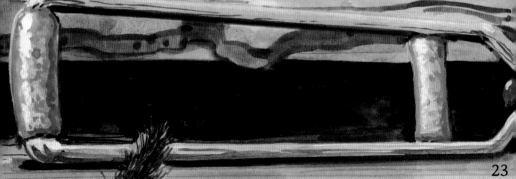

As the summer goes on, Henry's ankle becomes stronger. Soon he is well enough to go outside and play with Patches in the backyard. Patches is happy to play with Henry again!

At the end of the summer, Henry and his family decide to take a special trip to the beach . . . and they bring Patches!

The sun shines brightly, and the beach stretches farther than Patches can see. Patches loves to jump in the sand and chase the water as it comes up onto the shore.

After their vacation at the beach, Patches and his family go back home. Patches is excited to be back. He and Henry can run around in their big, fenced yard again. Patches loves his new house, his nice family and his best friend, Henry. Patches is so happy he was adopted!

Pet Health and Safety Tips

• Like Patches, many dogs have different breeds in their family trees. Purebred dogs are bred to have a consistent appearance, but mixed-breed dogs (often called "mutts") hardly ever look the same.

• A veterinarian can help you select a dog based upon your lifestyle. For instance, large dogs need plenty of opportunities for exercise and long-haired dogs can require lots of grooming. The veterinarian may also recommend some good places where you can go to get your new pet.

• Just like you, a dog needs time to adjust to new surroundings and new people. Some dogs may seem a little uncomfortable at first, but with patience, training, and lots of gentle care, they can become wonderful companions.

GLOSSARY

Shelter: A safe place for homeless animals to live.

Adopt: To take responsibility for the care of a pet.

Vaccine: Substance given to an animal that helps the animal protect itself against disease.

Cast: A sturdy form made of plaster or other material that is used to immobilize a broken bone.

A Real-Life Pet Tale

Stanley is a seven-year-old Border Collie who, like Patches, lived in a shelter until his loving family adopted him.

When Stanley was a puppy he was given to an elderly lady as a gift, but she could not take care of Stanley, who was a very energetic puppy. She brought him to a shelter so he could be adopted by a nice family that could take better care of him. When he was nine months old, Stanley was adopted by Jim and Christine of Detroit, Michigan. Jim and Christine liked to go to the local shelter to look at the dogs. When Christine walked in and saw Stanley, she knew they would be very happy together. Stanley was adopted and brought home to his new family!